CAMERON IN THE GAP